for

Cameron

Copyright © 1999 by Amanda Leslie

All rights reserved.

CIP Data is available.

Published in the United States 1999 by Dutton Children's Books,
a division of Penguin Putnam Books for Young Readers,
345 Hudson Street, New York, New York 10014
http://www.penguinputnam.com/yreaders/index.htm

Originally published in Great Britain 1999 by Little Rocket Books,
an imprint of Magi Publications, London

Printed in Malaysia   First American Edition
ISBN 0-525-46182-5
2 4 6 8 10 9 7 5 3 1

Amanda Leslie

flappy waggy wiggly

Dutton Children's Books
New York

woof!

who h
wag
yello
and a
licky

as a

gy

w tail

sticky

tongue?

dog

who h
wrih
green
and
of t

as a

kly

body

a lot

eeth?

who a w

grey and flappy

trumpet!

has avy trunk big ears?

who fluffy tail fe and quacky)

has blue
athers
a beak?

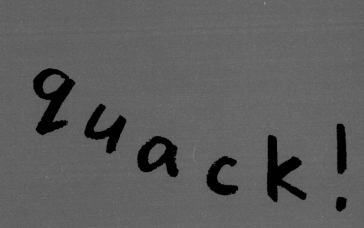

quack!

oink!

who h
snuf
pink
an
curly
ta

as a
fly
snout
d a
whirly
il?

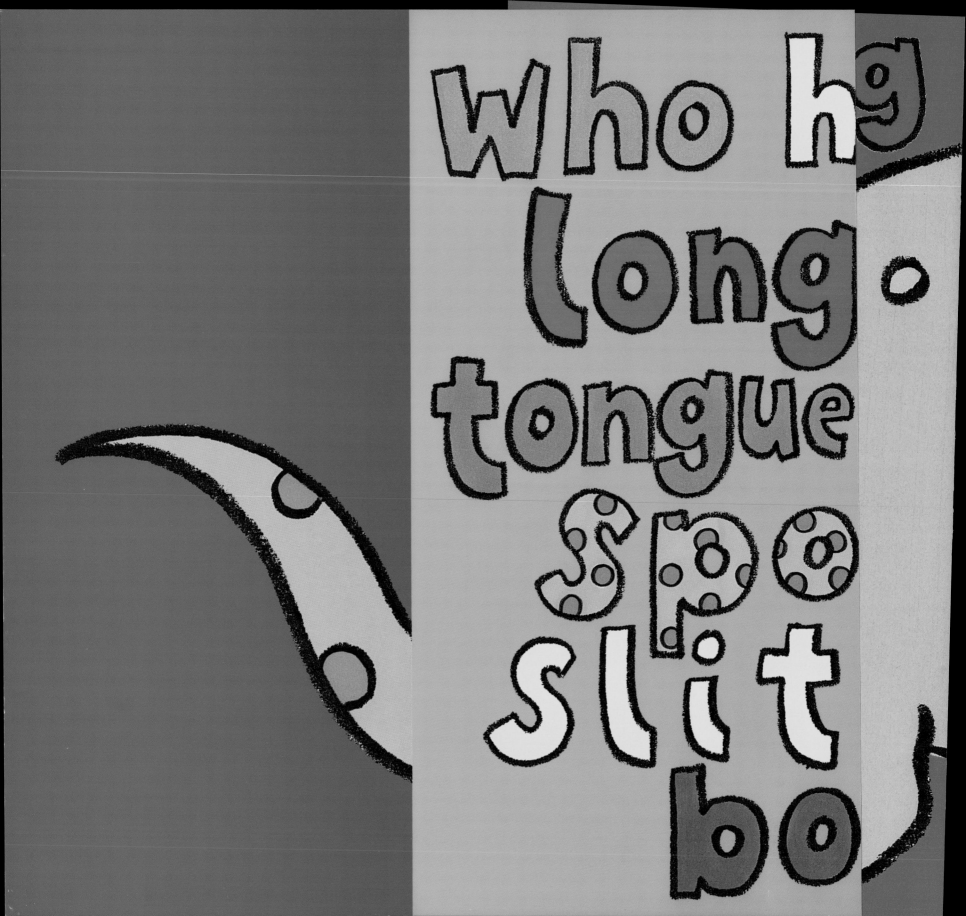

as a

ipy

e tail

big

kers?

as ten fingers iggly and s all noises?

e !

woof!

quack!

grrrow!!

hurroy!

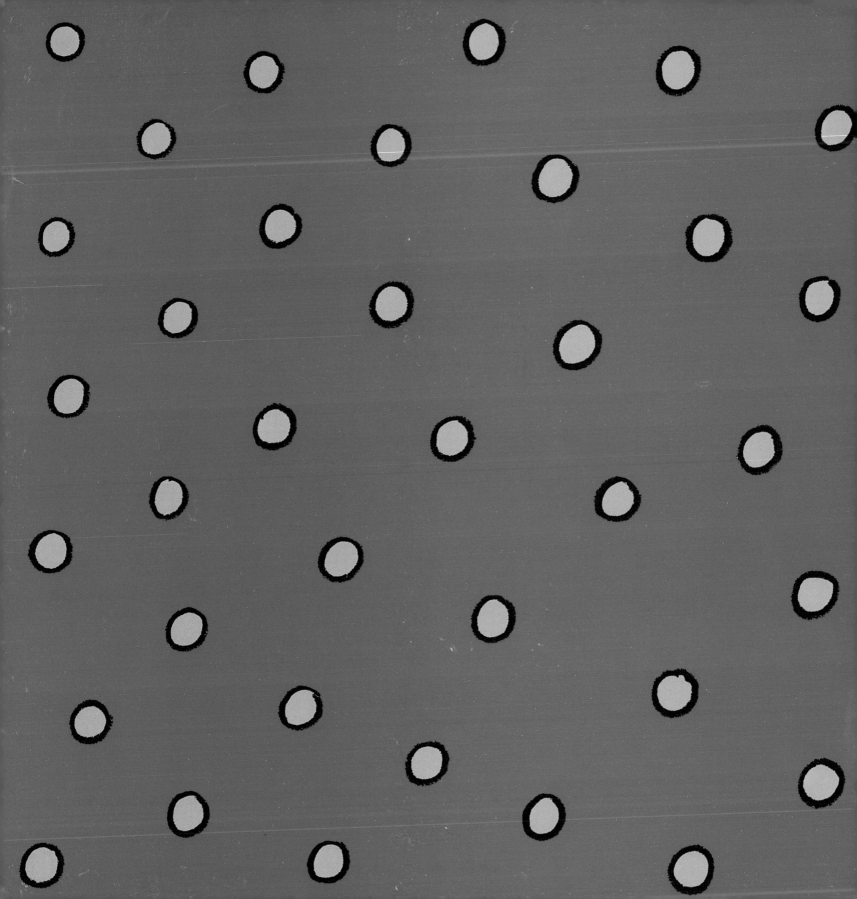